*For all those who face extraordinary mental
or physical challenges, and for their families
and caregivers, that in community we can
see one another in God's light*

THE BOOK OF
JOTHAM

ARTHUR POWERS

TUSCANY
PRESS LLC
WELLESLEY, MASSACHUSETTS
www.TuscanyPress.com

Tuscany Press, LLC
Wellesley, Massachusetts
www.TuscanyPress.com

Publisher's Cataloging-in-Publication Data
(Prepared by The Donohue Group, Inc.)

Powers, Arthur G.
  The book of Jotham / Arthur G. Powers.

    p. ; cm.

  ISBN: 978-1-939627-00-1

  1. People with mental disabilities--Religious life—Fiction. 2. Apostles—Fiction. 3. Jesus Christ—Fiction. 4. Faith—Fiction. 5. Catholic fiction. I. Title.

PS3616.O94 B66 2013
813/.6   2013930213

Printed and bound in the United State of America

10   9   8   7   6   5   4   3   2   1

Text design and layout by Peri Swan
This book was typeset in Garamond Premier Pro

Preface

In 1979, while living in Brazil, I became deeply concerned about the mentally disabled and their role in God's plan. I had until then been very much the kind of person who overvalues his mind, considering my intelligence to be the center of my being. The presence of mentally disabled people challenged me, frightened me.

For several weeks, I brought this matter to prayer. Then one morning, as I prayed in Our Lady of Mercy Chapel in Rio de Janeiro, the story of Jotham was given to me.

Research and writing followed, but the story presented here is the story born that day in prayer.

THE BOOK OF
JOTHAM

LIGHT OR DARKNESS. Warmth or cold.

You know them. Feel them.

The fire in black night. The afternoon sun in winter. The hoe handle, hard and grained in your large palms, moving up and down in your father's field. Up and down. Up and down.

"Not just over there, boy. Move along."

Father's anger. Not dark or cold, but hurt like a wounded dog, snapping out with sharp teeth. Hurting you inside.

"Lord, how have I sinned to have such a son?"

"Shh, Judah. It's no sin . . ."

"Silence, Sarah."

"The boy loves us, Judah. He's from God."

Mother. Lightest light. Warmest warmth. When you are near her, you feel inside like the shade of grape leaves on a spring day. Cool water in the well. Small sparrows in the air.

Where she goes, you follow. She bakes bread at the fire and sings. You smile. She turns and smiles up at you, her brown eyes warm and soft.

Until one day she's gone.

"She's dead," your sister says. "She won't come back."

Adina's eyes glisten wet. You are sitting on a mat and she is leaning over, in front of you, her face looking into yours. Her thin hands tighten hard on your shoulders. She shakes you.

"Do you understand?"

You move your head up and down, and she goes away. Up and down, goes your head, up and down. You feel dark and cold, so dark and cold, there will never be anything else. You stand up and look for your mother. She is not by the fire. You go outside. The fence, the field. "Ma . . . Mama!" you call. "Ma . . . Mama!"

She isn't there. The sun is empty and cold. The wind is dark, so dark.

"Mama!"

"Stop it! Stop it!"

Adina screams in front of you. She looks up at you, angry like the hurt dog. Her thin hands stretch out. Her screams hurt you inside. Drops of water run down her cheeks from her hurting eyes.

Father is no longer angry. He is only very, very far away. Not dark, but gray like a rain sky. His cold is not winter cold, only cold like when the fire is dead. He sits at the table. Hunched over. You stand up and walk to him. You put your big hand on his shoulder.

"Ab . . . Ab . . . Abba." The word is hard to say.

"Go away, boy."

"Ab . . . Abba."

Father stands up. He is angry. He looks at you, but then his eyes are not angry any more. Only far away. He puts his hand on your shoulder. Then he turns and walks out the door.

No more light and warmth. Dark, cold. Empty. You walk around, looking for your mother, but you don't call her name because Adina will be angry.

Days pass. Empty days. Father is far away. Your sister feeds you, but she isn't warm. She doesn't sing at the fire. You walk out of the house. Empty fields.

You go to the road. Light brown, sandy in the sunlight. You walk along the road, watching your bare feet follow the sandy tracks. Up and down, your feet walk. Up and down.

Voices. You look up. The village. White buildings in white sunlight. Bright sunlight that hurts your eyes. People. Noise. Don't go to the village, boy. You don't like the village. Dead meat hanging in doorways. Flies. People.

"Look who's here!"

Young man smiling at you. Not warm.

"Jotham." He says your name. "Idiot boy," he sings. Other young men, laughing. "Big as a house, stupid as a donkey."

Laugh again and again. Close. Yellow teeth. Bad breath. A hand pushes you, and you almost fall down. Laughter.

An old man in dark clothing. Quiet, hard voice. Angry. Not angry at you. Warm. Long dark robe, gray beard. The young men go away.

"Go home, boy," the old man says. Kind. Then you are alone.

No light. No warmth. But the sun is harsh, bright, and hot. You walk to a shaded place and sit down.

Mama, all the world is cold and dark, cold and dark. Where are you, Mama?

Every day you come and sit in this spot. The young men don't notice you now. People go by, talking. You watch them. Cold. Cold, empty, and dark.

Until one day you feel something new. People, lots of people, and their voices hum loud in the air. Bees in sunlight. You see people coming around the corner, a crowd of people.

And from them comes light. The lightest light you've ever known, but not bright to hurt your eyes. The warmest warmth, but not hot, not smoky, not cruel.

You stand up. The crowd passes. Your heart beats, up and down. You lift your feet, following the people. They seem far ahead, moving fast, but you follow.

Mile after mile. Out into the country, the dry fields on either side of the road. You've never walked so far. Your bare feet, up and down on the rocky ground, begin to hurt.

Far ahead is an open place with trees. A little river. More people than you've ever seen. When you reach them, they do not bother you or notice you. They are looking toward the light. You want to go to the light, but they stand, shoulder to shoulder, blocking your way.

Moments pass. There is only one sound, a man's voice, one warmth and one light. Then the voice stops and the people begin to turn away, as if there was no light.

"What did he say?" they ask. "What did he say?"

You push forward, among the people talking, turning away. And then you see the light.

It isn't mother. It isn't a woman. It is a man. He stands under a tree, talking to several young men who listen, eager. He is not facing you. You approach him from the side, a little bit from behind, and you get very close. You hear his strong voice, see his dark hair and beard, light-colored robe, muscular brown hands. He is not your mother. You cannot call him Mama.

And then you know. "Abba," you say quietly.

He wheels around and looks at you with startled, knowing eyes.

"AB . . . BA."

"Why do you call me that?" he asks.

"Abba," you say again.

He probes you with his clear brown eyes.

Then, softly, "What's your name?"

"Jo . . . Jo-tham."

His eyes are not like Mama's eyes. They are farther away, yet nearer, so near they go right inside you. They make you feel shy.

"Do you want to go with us, Jotham?"

5

You move your head up and down, then faster, up and down.

"Come then," he says.

You walk for miles and miles, following him. There is no crowd now, only a few men and women. Young men walk with him, talking. You walk behind, following the light. The world is light, warm and light.

The sun sets, but still the light glows ahead. He shines brightly in the growing dark.

They stop by a river. Firelight. Soft sounds. A young woman comes up to you. She gives you a bowl of food. You hold the bowl. Smooth. Flat, smooth bread is pressed into your hand. Warm food in your mouth, warm in your throat, warm in your belly.

"My name is Mary," the young woman says. "What's yours?"

"Jo . . . Jo-tham."

"Here. Let me wipe your face."

Cool, damp cloth on your face. Soft hands, brown eyes. Firelight.

"Your feet!"

You see your feet in firelight. Caked bloody. Up and down, up and down on the rocky road. Hurt.

She goes to the river. She comes back. Large brown cloth. She leans down. Long dark hair. Pretty. Cool, wet cloth on your feet, softly, softly.

This new Abba whom you can't call Abba. In the night, you wake and he is kneeling close beside you. Moonlight touches his face, but he is light. Lightest light that does not hurt your eyes. Your heart sings inside you, fire song, open field song, bright winter air. You laugh.

He smiles. He is looking again into your eyes. A long time.

"Father. Why have you sent him to me?" he asks. His voice is questioning, soft.

You wait. Your heart leaps toward the light. It sings. It dances for the light.

"Jotham. Can you hear me?"

You move your head up and down. Up and down.

"Stop." Gentle voice. His hand holds your chin. Strong fingers. Callused, rough, and comforting.

"Look at me."

Your eyes find his. His eyes see inside you, making you shy.

"Call me Jesus."

Sunlight on your eyelids. Glowing red. Voices. You open your eyes and see green grass by the river. Blue sky. White clouds.

Your heart is dancing. Your body lifts up, strong, good. You walk to the river, into the river. Cool water on your legs. Cool water on your thighs, stomach, chest. You dip your face. Cool. Wet.

You turn. He is standing on the bank. He sees you. He smiles.

Mary feeds you. You sit on the ground.

A big man. Bigger than any man you've ever seen, and solid. He kneels in front of you. Smiles. Big nose, beard, crooked teeth. Kind eyes.

"I'm Peter, Jotham. They call me the rock."

"Should be the mountain!" someone says. They laugh. Peter laughs. Happy laugh, not hurting. You laugh, too.

"See, Thomas. Our friend thinks you're funny," Peter calls out.

"Judas always says my humor is fit for a simpleton."

Second man. Kneels beside Peter. Brown, curly hair. No beard. Face makes you smile, laugh.

"He even likes my face."

"This is Thomas, Jotham," Peter says, pointing his thumb. "Do the sandals fit?" Thomas asks.

"Haven't tried yet." Peter holds out a sandal. "Let's put this on, Jotham."

Leather. Hard and smooth against your foot.

"Fine. A little big, but you'll be able to walk farther tomorrow."

"Your sandals are the only ones that would fit him. Look at those feet."

"I'll lace them for you." Peter smiles. Leather straps, tight around your leg. Tight, sharp, strong.

People are coming. Crowds of people. New Abba, Jesus, makes them sit on the ground. He stands and talks. Clear voice, strong. You sit in the warmth and light, letting the warmth and light flow over you, through you.

The sun climbs high in the sky. Sweat trickles down your side and back. Good sweat.

The sun is hot, but it cannot hurt you. The other light protects you, makes the sun safe and small.

The voice stops. People turn away. They do not see the light. He is close to you.

"Je . . . sus," you say. "Je . . . sus." The word feels good on your tongue.

"Yes, Jotham?" His eyes are smiling.

Your dancing heart bows down inside you. Hail to him . . . it sings . . . Hail to him . . . Blessed is he who comes in the name . . .

His eyes are smiling into you.

"Jotham," Mary says quietly, "you must call him Rabbi. It shows respect. You can't call him Jesus."

"Let him be, Mary." Mary spins around. Abba is behind her. Light.

"But, Rabbi . . ."

"He can call me Jesus." Smiles into your eyes. "He knows who I am."

"HOW CAN WE BAPTIZE HIM, Rabbi? He understands nothing."

Morning. Cool sunlight, blue sky. The river in front of you. The light.

"What makes you say that, Peter? Because he doesn't talk?"

"Talk? His eyes are dull as dust."

"Yet he knows more than most."

Peter leans over and peers into your eyes.

"He's like that, Rabbi?"

Abba laughs.

"Are you still looking for it in his eyes, Peter?"

"Yes, Rabbi."

"Look in his heart."

You walk into the river. Peter beside you. Others behind you. Cold water on your legs, on your thighs, stomach, chest. Peter's hand holds you. He turns you toward him.

Peter's face. Stern. Strong. Eyes on you. You are afraid. He talks. You are cold, afraid. His words sound bright and hard, deep in your chest.

He is looking at you. Not talking. Hands on your shoulders.

"Say yes, Jotham."

"Yes."

"Don't be afraid."

Hands push you down. Water. You can't see, can't breathe. Abba, Abba. Your arms lash out. Hands bring you up. Air. Bright sky. Push you down. Terror. Abba, help me. Eyes blind, water breath. Struggle. Hands bring you up. Air. Light. Push you down. Blind. Dead. Do not struggle. Abba, save me. Hands bring you up. Arms hold you. Peter's arms, Mary's arms. Walking, water going down. Walking onto land.

Abba. He smiles.

Mary close beside you, whispering, "Now you are one of us."

"What are we becoming? A vagabond troupe? First women, now idiots?"

Firelight. Clear gray eyes. Clean-cut, handsome face.

"Is it beneath your dignity, Judas, to walk with vagabonds?" Clear gray eyes turn away.

"Sorry, Thomas. I forgot to mention clowns."

"Huzzah!" Thomas leaps in the air, lands, and bows. Makes a face. You laugh. "A sharp compliment, Judas."

Judas laughs. "The idiot likes your capers, Thomas. I always said . . ."

"I know, I know, brother. But what about our vagabond troupe? Clown, if you like, tax collector, zealot? . . ."

"What's all this?" Peter's voice. Peter walking into the firelight.

"Not to mention fishermen. I almost forgot fishermen."

"What about fishermen?" Peter squats by the fire.

"Nothing. Thomas is playing. I only said I didn't see why we have to tow along an idiot."

"And women," Thomas says.

"And women. Who will listen to us if they don't respect

us? Women were bad enough, but this fellow doesn't even understand. And that baptism—he was scared half to death in the water."

Peter poked the fire with a stick. "I know. It doesn't make sense. But the rabbi wants it that way."

"The rabbi's not in this world." Judas's quiet voice. "Unless we help him, he will make a fool of himself."

"What is it you want, Judas? That Jotham utter words of praise?"

Abba. Abba's voice. You leap up. Thomas and Judas leap up. Peter stays poking the fire.

You cannot see Abba, but you feel the light.

"Rabbi?" Judas says.

Abba walks into the firelight.

"I asked only what you want, Judas. Would you feel better if Jotham sang praises to our Lord?"

"Rabbi, I only wanted to know how he could understand, and how he could be baptized . . ."

"Jotham!" Abba's voice. His eyes on you, not deep, but commanding.

Then your lips open. Praise God! say your lips, Praise God. Glory to God in the highest. Praise him heaven and earth, sun and stars praise him. Praise him!

Your lips stop. Light glows in you. Peter, Judas, Thomas stare at you.

"Is he cured, Rabbi?"

"Cured, Thomas? Was he sick?"

Silence. Abba looks at Judas.

"Well, Judas?"

"It is enough, Rabbi. I don't understand."

"I thought it was Jotham who doesn't understand." Abba puts his hand on Judas's shoulder. "No, you don't understand, Judas. Our God says, 'It is not those who cry out "Lord! Lord!" who will be saved. It is those who live my way.'"

Abba turns. Walks out of the firelight. But still the light glows. Tired. Up and down. Feet up and down all day.

Thomas comes close. Looks at you. "What's your name?"

"Jo . . . Jo-tham."

"He hasn't changed, Peter."

"Let me see."

Peter places his hands on your shoulders. Turns you toward the fire. Looks into your eyes. Careful. Long.

"Dull as dust," he says.

WHITE EYEBALLS, pupils half rolled up into his head. Blind eyes. Man like a hurt dog, crouched in the dust. White lice crawl in his dark, caked hair. He paws the air with his hands.

Abba standing beside you. You feel hurt in his heart, great gaping pain. Reaching, reaching toward the hurt dog blind man.

The man's mouth opens. Withered, black teeth. Foul

breath. Old rags, sweated dirty, hang around his thin body.

Abba hurting. The light. Reaching. Reaching.

The man's lips move. Painful.

"Master."

"Yes?"

Silence. The man's mouth. Beggar's mouth, whining. Sweat beading his forehead. Thin body glistening sweat.

"Teach me to see."

Abba's hand reaching out. Touching the blind man's hair. Light. The blind man sweats. Light. Brighter, brighter. Flickering.

"Your faith has healed you."

The man's eyes roll right. You see his eyes, foggy. Glazed, then growing bright. His hands paw the air, then stop. He looks around, then slowly stands, staggering like a drunk man. He looks at Abba. Hurt dog. Afraid.

"Go in peace. Tell no one."

He stares at Abba. Seeing eyes. Forever. He stares at Abba forever and ever. Afraid. He breaks his eyes away and turns and scurries off, afraid. Hurt dog.

Abba tired. Tired. His face hot, wet. The light glowing.

Thomas beside you. His laughing face stilled.

"Rabbi, you didn't cure Jotham, but you cured the blind man."

Firelight. Abba squatting, drawing on the ground with a stick. Thomas, Judas, Peter sitting on the ground.

"Jotham doesn't need to be cured, Thomas."

"But the blind man did?"

Abba traces. Soft sound of stick in dirt.

"We're not here to change the outer, Thomas. We're here to change the inner."

"But, Rabbi, the blind man saw!"

Abba looks up. He holds his stick in one hand, slapping it gently against the open palm of the other. Tap. Tap.

"Yes, he saw. And when he saw, the blindness fell away. When you change the inner, the outer changes of its own accord."

"Then we can cure all blindness, Rabbi." Judas's voice.

"Some men have blind eyes but see. Others have seeing eyes but are blind. We can't cure all blindness of the heart, Judas. And we don't need to cure all blindness of the eyes."

Silence. Abba's stick, soft in the dirt. Abba's eyes watching the stick trace patterns under firelight.

"But, Rabbi." Thomas's voice. "A blind man has a mind to see with. How can Jotham see?"

Abba watching his stick. The stick taps the ground. Up and down. Up and down. Tap. Tap. Tap.

"Do you want to hear a story, Thomas?"

"Will it answer my question, Rabbi?"

Abba watching the ground, smiles a big smile. Tap. Tap. Tap. The stick stops.

"A certain potter made four pots," Abba says. He stands up, stretches his legs. Then he sits on the ground, hands back to support him, legs straight in front. He looks at Judas.

"One is beautifully made. Smooth, symmetrical, the kind of pot you find in a rich man's home.

"The potter fills it with water, and it holds the water well. Until one day, he fills it a little more. It bursts apart, and all the water is lost."

Abba sits up, crosses his legs. Picks up his stick. He looks at Thomas.

"The second pot is comical. People smile when they see it. But it holds water well except . . ."

Abba looks down, smiles. Draws a line with the stick.

"Except it keeps spouting little leaks here and there. Not enough to do much harm, but the potter has to keep patching it with wax."

Silence. Firelight.

"And the others, Rabbi?" Judas's voice. Cold.

"The third is a big pot. Truly, the biggest you'd want to see." Abba looks at Peter. Abba's eyes sparkle. "And serviceable. You can pour lots of water into it, except . . ."

"Except?" Peter asks.

"Except it's porous. It always loses a little of the water, drips a little. You know that kind of pot, Peter?"

"I know that kind, Rabbi."

"Good. And the fourth pot. It's awkward, ugly, misshapen, thick. But you can pour water into it, and pour, and it never leaks or cracks or bursts."

Abba stands up. Tired. Throws away the stick.

Silence. Abba turns, walks out of the firelight. Judas stands.

16

Walks away.

Quiet. Thomas looks at you. Looks at the fire.

"I still don't see why all the pots can't be strong and beautiful."

Firelight. You are tired. Heavy body, heavy eyes.

Peter shrugs.

"Maybe it's God's way."

UP AND DOWN. Up and down.

Day after day, you walk, following him. Dry country. Stony roads. The big sandals Peter gave you, up and down in the dust. You stumble, fall. Pain, red blood flowing. Mary puts water on your knees, washes away the blood.

Day after day. You've never gone so far. Green fields. Men and boys staring from the fields, women staring from the doors of houses. Villages. Rivers. A big water that glitters. Up and down, up and down.

People. People coming to see the light. They hear the words but do not see the light. When he stops talking, they turn away.

Some follow. They walk with you, and ask: "What's this, an idiot?"

"We call him simple," Mary says.

"An idiot studying with a rabbi?" Laughter.

"The rabbi loves him."

Night. A village. A house where men and women talk quietly. Abba is gone.

"He's nearby, Jotham," Mary says. "In another house." You see his light flickering in her face, you feel him in the men and women around you.

A young woman serves you food. She looks at you out of the corner of her eye. Children look at you, quietly. You laugh and hold out your hand to them. They laugh and back away.

"He won't hurt them?"

"Hurt them? He's gentle as a lamb."

"But he's big. He looks as though he could break them in half."

"He's strong, but he doesn't hurt anyone."

Men eating. The quiet of dipping and chewing.

"Why would your rabbi bring along a big child like that?"

Night. An open place. A few low fires. You cannot see Abba, but you know he isn't far away.

You sleep. Jagged dreams. Old Abba in your old house, sitting at the table. You put your hand on his shoulder. He stands up, looks at you, turns away. Abba! Abba!

Your sleep fills with light. You open your eyes.

New Abba. Beside you. Sitting on the ground.

His eyes far away. His face peaceful, glowing. He sees something.

You lie still and watch. Mama. Cooking fire. Singing, singing.

Your sleep fills with light.

18

Afternoon. Sunlight, a brushy field, trees. A river winding by.

Hot air, cooling. You sit by the new-lit fire. Tired legs. Voices in quiet air.

"Hey! . . ." Peter's voice. Thomas laughing and running. He stops, looks back at Peter. Peter standing up, mud in his hair. He brushes grass from his tunic.

"If that's what you want! . . ." Peter strides to the riverbank. Long, strong strides. He stoops and pulls with his hand. He stands again, his hand holding grass and mud. "Thomas!" he calls.

"I can hear you from here." Thomas laughs.

Peter starts running toward Thomas. Thomas laughs, ducks, and dodges. Big Peter, running heavy. Little Thomas, quick and light. You laugh and hear others laugh. Mary's pretty laugh. You look and see her caught up in joy.

Thomas standing near the trees. Peter swings back his arm and throws the mud. Thomas ducks. Abba steps from among the trees.

"Rabbi!" Peter's voice. Silence.

Abba stands with mud splattered on his tunic.

"Rabbi, I didn't mean . . ."

Abba laughing inside. You see his eyes, far away but close, laughing, and you laugh aloud.

"Jotham!" Mary says.

But Abba is laughing inside. He leans over and picks up a clod of earth from the ground. "Here, Peter!" He tosses it.

Peter holds up his hands and catches the clod. It breaks in

his hands, splattering dry earth in all directions.

Peter looks at Abba, startled. Then they both burst out laughing.

"And Thomas?" Peter says.

"Ah . . . Thomas is too quick." Abba laughs. "I could never catch him."

Abba starts walking toward the fire. He sees you and smiles a laughing smile.

"Here, Jotham." He leans down, picks up a clod of damp earth. Gently he swings, and the clod arches through the air toward you.

You hold out your hands, and suddenly the damp clod is in your hands with a soft smack. It fits perfectly in your hands, a living sphere of grass and earth.

Night. A dry place. You wake. Cold, crisp air. Bright stars. Hard ground. You sit up. You watch, listen. Black land, sleeping figures, embers. The rustle of sleepers.

The light.

You stand up. You feel the light in the distance. You walk. Your bare feet taste the hard ground with joy.

You walk away from camp. Among rocks and small, twisted trees. Then you see him standing against the starred sky. The light glows brightly, dims, glows more brightly, again and again.

You stop and sit on the hard ground and watch. Waiting.

Glory to God, sings your heart. Praise him! Praise him!

20

Glory to God . . . Blessed is he . . .

You wait and you watch and the sky grows gray, pale silver, glowing bright.

❋❋

A HAND SHAKING YOU. Bright sky. You open your eyes.

Mary standing over you. Long dark hair; gentle face; pretty brown eyes.

"What are you doing out here, Jotham? I was looking for you."

You smile, and she smiles back.

"Come on, you big lug. I don't know why I worry about you."

She walks off, and you get up. You look to where he stood last night, but he is gone.

Where is the light? Where is the light?

You walk among the men, looking. Talking. Laughter. A man on the ground rolling up a blanket. Peter. Judas.

There is no light.

Gray. Gray under the bright sun. You look among the women. Talking. Laughter. Clay pots. Mary.

He isn't there.

You sit down. Empty. Wait here, he will be back. Gray. Tired.

"Let's go, Jotham." Peter's voice.

You sit. Wait here. Gray. Tired.

"Jotham, we're moving on. Mary, what's wrong with Jotham? Is he sick?"

Mary comes over. She looks at you.

"This morning, I found him asleep way out over there."

"What's going on?" Judas's voice.

"Something's wrong with Jotham."

Judas's clear gray eyes.

"What's wrong, Jotham?"

You look at him. Where is the light?

"He misses the rabbi," Judas says.

"Of course." Peter's voice is happy. "Hey, Jotham. The rabbi will be back. He's gone up into the hills. He'll be meeting us at Capernaum."

"Come on, Jotham," Mary says. "We have to go meet the rabbi."

She smiles. Warmth. Kindness. Dim, dim light. You tense your legs and stand up.

"He really feels when the rabbi's gone." Peter's voice, quiet, talking of a new great thing.

Fear.

A village. White buildings close on a narrow street. You remember. People. Noise.

You stand. Mary beside you. Alone. Three men in front of you. Red eyes, stubbled chins. Strong breath.

"I know this woman!"

"Please, let us pass." Mary's voice is soft, scared.

"Let you pass? Why, don't you remember me? Where was it, Caesarea? I said I was your love forever." Laughter. "How about a kiss for your love."

Mary looks at the ground. "Please, let us pass."

"What is this? Pass without a kiss?"

Laughter. Women in the windows. Men lolling in the street.

"Someone said to me, 'There are women along with these prophets preaching love.' Ooh, I want some of that love."

Laughter. The man staggers forward and grabs Mary's arm.

Red-hot iron. Sharp. An animal in your chest you never felt before. Your hands find the man's tunic, grab him, lift him in the air.

"Jotham, stop!"

You lift him high in the air. Your muscles strong, feeling good. You throw. He falls hard against the stone street.

"Jotham!" Mary pulls back your arm. She steps forward. The other two men draw knives. Sharp. Glinting sunlight.

Mary stoops by the hurt man. She is between you and the men with knives. They look at her and look at you.

"He's alive. Bring vinegar."

You stand still. The knives relax. A woman comes from a house. A small bowl, a sponge. Mary places the sponge on the man's head, then on his lips. Her own lips move soundlessly. The man's eyes open.

She sponges his face again, then rises and steps back.

The men with knives stand watching. The hurt man

moves, then sits up. Slowly. Painfully, he gets to his feet.

"Forgive us," Mary says.

The man looks at her. Strangely. He nods his head, very slightly.

She comes and takes your hand and you start walking. She leads you through the men holding knives, then down the street.

DIM. ALMOST GRAY. Abba has not come back.

Rain. Your sandals, up and down on mud roads.

Mud and water, smooth and cool on your feet. Rainwater on your head, arms, trickling down your neck.

Sunlight. Green fields, bright sky. Yet still the light has not come.

In villages, men gather and Peter talks. Not the light, but a dim glow. Men listen, ask questions. Sometimes Peter answers, sometimes Thomas, sometimes Judas.

"Judas is the cleverest of us," Peter tells Mary.

Water on the ground.

You look down. Brown water. Still as stone.

Sky in the water. Clouds. Blue sky looks blue-brown. White clouds look white-brown. Birds fly in the water, far below.

Face in the water. Your face, Jotham's face. Large. Soft. Flat nose. Brown-gold skin in brown water. Brown, dull eyes in brown, dull water.

A dim, dim glow.

Clear gray eyes. Judas's voice. Kind.

"What do you think about, Jotham?"

Confusion. Smoke in your head, behind your eyes.

"Our rabbi can do many things. He made your lips praise God."

Smoke in your head. Singing. Praise God . . .

"But I wonder what's in your heart."

Dim. Gray. Abba, where are you?

"Sometimes I look at your face and I think you don't know anything. Then sometimes I think you see more than I do."

His eyes watch you. Circling smoke. Confusion. He smiles.

"Well, you can't answer questions for me, can you?" He smiles again and looks away. "It's like the rabbi. Where is he taking us, eh, Jotham? Is he going to let all his powers just trickle away in Galilee? Leading a few peasants and women?" He laughs, then looks back at you, reaches out, and touches your arm. "And an idiot, Jotham. We can't forget that."

Still water. Brown. Dark, deep water. His mind is a sharp knife cutting deep water.

"I don't understand, Jotham. Maybe you do, but I don't."

Silence. Deep water. Judas's quiet voice.

"When is our rabbi going to start doing God's work?"

NEW FACES.

"We're in Capernaum, Jotham," Mary says. "The rabbi will meet us here."

New faces. Matthew. Dark. Deep lines, sad eyes. John. Gentle. Quiet smile, distant, warm eyes. Philip, Andrew, Nathaniel. Young. Strong faces.

"She came with you?" Mary asks.

"Yes. From Nazareth." Philip answers.

Mary walks beside you, talking with the others. In front of you, a small house. Old walls, no longer white. A small, square window.

You stop. The window of the house glows. Not the light, but a soft, steady glow.

"Come on, Jotham." Mary's voice pulls you.

You walk. Your heart is quiet. Waiting.

Mary walks through the door. You follow. A table.

Women.

A woman seated near the table. Graying hair, olive skin, dark brown eyes. Old clothes. Hard-worked feet, hard-worked hands.

Mama. Not old Mama, who is gone, but new Mama. Glowing, warm singing at the fire.

Mama, Mama. You are on your knees, your head on her lap. Her hand strokes your hair.

"Jotham, get up! This is the rabbi's mother."

"Let him be, Mary," the woman says.

GLOW. DAYS GLOW with this new mother. People come to talk to her. Old men, old women, young women ripe with child.

Sometimes she only listens. Sometimes she talks softly. Sometimes her voice is firm, or her eyes fill with tears, or she begins to laugh.

You can't always be with her. Mary leads you off. She gives you pots to clean. Round and round you rub. Round and round.

"Hey, Jotham." Thomas's eyes dance. "That must be the cleanest pot in Galilee."

"Leave him alone!" Mary's sharp voice.

Round and round. Round and round. Glow. Quiet. Round and round.

Waiting for the light.

"Ma . . . ary!"

"What is it, Jotham?"

You take her hand. Your legs want to run. Your heart wants to dance.

"Ma . . . ary!"

You pull her hand.

"What does he want?" Peter's voice.

"I don't know." Mary's voice, puzzled. You dance, your heart dances. She smiles, laughs.

The light. The light.

"I don't know, but I suppose we'd better go with him." She starts to walk. Peter walks with her. You run ahead, looking back.

"We're coming." Peter's voice laughing. The light.

You feel it coming, far away.

Run. Your feet run over the cobblestones. Light. Flying. Dirt road, scattered houses. Run, run.

Your heart hurts. You hear it panting. Walk. Walk on and on. The road, the fields, a hill.

You see him.

He shines, all golden and bright.

You run again, your heart hurting.

First, you think he is alone. Then you see the others with him. Men. Women. Children. Walking in his light.

And he is laughing. Laughing and leading them. Shining. Golden.

You stop running and stand. Wait, shining inside. Mary comes up beside you, and Peter.

"A king," she whispers, and she lays her hand on your arm.

SUNLIGHT THROUGH the square window. A square of light on the wooden table. Abba's hands within the light, his face in shadow.

The men sit around the large table. Only his mother, of all the women, sits. She sits beside him. Other women stand.

Children. You stand.

Abba's hands are in the light. His face is in shadow. But he is light. Bright light.

All morning he has been speaking. Men ask him questions, and he answers. The words are long and hard. You hear them but you don't remember them. You watch the light and are happy.

A rustle of sound. Women bring food into the room: large bowls and loaves of bread. Bread is thrust at you.

A young girl stands with her arm out. Bread in her hand. Her eyes. Rabbit's eyes. Wide open, scared. Your big hand takes the bread. Flat and hard. The girl scurries away.

You hold the bread in your hand. Bring it to your mouth. Your teeth tear it. You taste the grainy, good flavor. Warm. Safe. You're Mama's good boy, Jotham.

Chewing. Chewing. The good bread filling your mouth, softened, moistened, then growing dry.

Someone passes wine. You feel the cup in your hand, then lift it to your mouth. Wine spills from the cup into your mouth, touching the bread, making it soft again, alive. Wine trickles on your lips, your chin. You lower the cup and your head. Chewing. You wipe your face with your hand.

Sunlight and wild grass. Hot sun and gentle breeze. A hillside and, far below, blue sea.

You lie on your back close to Abba. You feel safe. Abba's words flow around you, flow to the others close by you, flow out to the crowd. The crowd sits in the light, reflecting the light.

Abba's strong words flowing out to the people, flowing, then slowing, slowing. Grayness flickers through the crowd. Restless. The reflection of the light dims in the people.

"Rabbi, the people are growing hungry. Let them go to the villages and buy food."

Sunlight. Rustling movement. An emptiness in you.

"Feed them with what you have."

"But Rabbi, we can't possibly feed all these people."

"What food do you have?"

Sunlight. Rustling. Murmuring voices, soft against the brush. An emptiness in you, a good clean emptiness.

"There's a boy here with five loaves of bread and a couple of fish. That's all."

"Bring them to me."

Rustling movement. Murmuring voices, soft against the wild grass. Silence. Abba's voice. Soft music rising, rising to beyond where you can see. Up, up goes your heart, up with Abba's voice, up beyond.

Abba's voice, clear and strong, offering blessings to God.

Sunlight, movement, murmuring. Sounds of those you love around you. Philip's voice, close by.

"Sit up, Jotham. Have some bread."

You lift yourself, sitting up. Waking. Newness.

Philip breaks a small piece of bread and gives you half. You look into his eyes. Clear, dark, peaceful. You take the bread and put it in your mouth. Good, full. Living.

Philip has turned away. A boy comes toward you, holding a piece of bread. You swallow the last of the bread in your mouth. You look at the boy. He smiles. Breaks the bread and hands it to you. Walks away. Bread in your hand. Hungry. Ready to eat.

A little girl. Large brown eyes watching the bread about to go into your mouth. You stop. Her eyes, brown and deep. You break the bread, give her part. She takes it, smiles at you, runs away.

Your teeth in the good bread. You bite a mouthful and chew. You close your eyes. Your heart, up, up, beyond.

"Jotham." You open your eyes. Mary. She hands you a piece of fish. Smiles. Her eyes are happy, close and far away, new and clear, the clearness you saw beyond.

Mary walks on to others, sharing the fish. You look at your hands. Fish in one hand, bread in the other.

You bite the bread and then the fish. You close your eyes, chewing. Crisp fish, living bread. You feel cooling sunlight, you hear rustling movement, murmuring voices. Crisp fish. Full, grainy, living bread. Love.

You eat and the emptiness fills. You lie back on the brush. You feel a small piece of bread still in your hand. Peaceful, filled, glowing. Happy.

Cool sunlight. Wild grass and a gentle breeze. Hillside. Far below, blue sea.

❀❀

"WHY DON'T YOU HELP us, Rabbi?"

The man's voice echoes out of the noise of the crowd toward Abba's back. Abba walking up the street, away from the crowd. He stops and turns slowly. A hush falls over the street. Beyond the crowd, the street slopes down to the sea.

The man who spoke stands in front of the crowd. Dark-haired, muscular. His face is a question.

Abba's voice, sharp. Speaking to a man in the crowd.

"You haven't come here because you believe in me. You've come because I gave you all you could eat."

The crowd is silent. The man stands dumb, looking at Abba.

Abba's voice again. Soft now.

"I wish you would think as much about feeding your souls as you do about feeding your bodies."

Abba turns, starts walking away.

"But, Rabbi!" The man calls out.

Abba stops. A bird in the blue sky.

The man's voice. "What are we supposed to do? What does God want?"

Silence. Abba turns back and takes a step toward the man. "Believe in me." Pleading. Abba's voice soft, but all hear.

Silence.

The man stands looking at Abba.

Another man's voice. "How are we to know? What sign will you give us? When Moses came, God sent manna for our fathers to eat. He sent them bread from heaven."

Silence.

Abba looks out over the crowd.

"I am the bread from heaven."

His voice is not loud, but it reaches to the edges of the square, down the street, to the water. You see it touch houses, walls. You see it touch the faces of the people.

The people stand dumb, staring at Abba.

"I am the bread of life. He who comes to me will never be hungry. He who believes in me will never thirst . . ."

Abba's voice goes on flowing over you. Light shining brightly. You listen, happy in his voice, in the light.

"Your fathers ate manna in the desert, and they died."

"I am the living bread. Who eats this bread will live forever."

The sun low in the sky. People turning away. Abba's voice flowing.

"The bread I shall give you is my flesh. I will give it for the life of the world."

"What is he saying, Peter?" Judas's voice, sharp in your ear.

"Unless you eat the flesh of the Son of Man and drink his blood, you will not have life."

You see the people's faces. Hurt, wondering. Like the hurt dog. They turn away.

"Those who eat my flesh and drink my blood abide in me, and I abide in them."

Dusk over the water. The empty square. The light, standing alone. A few people, lonely in the shadows. Peter walks toward Abba. Touches his arm.

"Rabbi, the people have gone."

Abba turns. Dusk. You see deep into his dark brown eyes.

"And you, Peter?" He looks beyond Peter. His voice is quiet, sad. "And you, Judas? Nathan? Philip—all of you? Will you leave me now too?"

Silence. A long silence. Dusk darkening. You hear lapping water, the echo of distant voices.

"Rabbi." Peter's voice. "Where would we go?"

"HOSANNA!"

Mary smiling. Men shouting, happy. Your heart dances. People, people around you, laughing. Palm leaves rustling the air. People seeing the light. Joy, joy, warm strong light of people.

Your feet dance. Up and down, higher and higher. Peter presses a palm leaf into your hand. "Dance, Jotham!"

Abba, the light, riding a donkey. People move aside to make a path. "Hosanna!" Palms rustling in air.

Abba. Happy among his laughing people.

"Jotham!" Judas's arm around you. His gray eyes bright and happy. "Look, Jotham. Jerusalem!" He points ahead. "Soon."

"What does he know of Jerusalem?" Thomas's voice. "He sees a king, don't you, Jotham?"

A king, a king.

"Not a king yet." Judas's voice. "But soon . . ."

A king, a king. The golden word inside you. You see Abba on the donkey. Abba golden. Light on his head. "A crown." Is that Thomas's voice or a voice inside you? "A golden crown."

Abba, all golden, riding on a donkey. Donkey. Soft, large brown eyes, eyes like your eyes. Your heart calls the donkey, calls Abba, calls Judas and Thomas and the people. Your feet dance on the stones of the road. Stones and palm leaves and sky dance with joy.

"Rabbi!" A tall, straight man in dark clothing. He walks through the crowd like a clean knife. Sharp words. "Rabbi. Control your people."

The people's laughter and cheers seem far away. You stand in silence between the tall, straight man and golden Abba. You and Judas and Thomas stand in silence in the roaring crowd. The moving, dancing palms sound like rain.

The tall, straight man and golden Abba. Abba laughs gently. His hand sweeps downward toward the stone-paved road. "If my people don't shout with joy, these stones will."

Silence. A moment. Thomas coming alive. Air flowing into his lungs. "Hosanna!" he shouts.

Your heart leaps alive and dances.

You've never seen so many people.

Street after street. Crowded. Bumping. Haggling. Laughing.

"Stay close to us, Jotham." Judas, Mary, Peter.

Market. Sunlight on bright-colored fruit. Meat hanging from poles. Flies. Sunlight on tanned leather.

Mary's eyes. Her smile. Your heart dancing within you.

Hawkers. Beggars. Fair-skinned men in light clothes. Dark-skinned men in flowing robes.

Warm sunlight.

"Stay close to us," Mary whispers.

Fear.

Tall, strange men. Helmets. Breastplates, swords. Strutting, proud, among the people.

Peter stops. You and the others stop with him. People around you talk, haggle, laugh. Peter stands silent, watching the tall, strange men. His muscles tense. Judas's eyes watching. Cat's eyes. Cold-flamed anger.

"What is it, Peter?" Mary's voice is soft.

Judas's sharp whisper. "He feels what I do. He can't stand to see those foreigners acting like lords in the holy city."

Peter turns around. "No." His eyes pass over you, meet Judas's eyes, then find Mary's. "I was suddenly afraid," he says.

Silence. Judas nods. "Of course. We're near the enemy and it's almost time. But you'll be all right when the time comes." His hand on Peter's arm. "You are our rock." He smiles.

They walk again. You follow. No more fear. But uneasiness. Heavy air.

"The time?" Mary's quiet voice.

Judas turns quickly. Almost whispering. Gray eyes dancing, excited, making you uneasy. "Great things will happen, Mary. You'll see." Then bursting. "You saw how the people followed the rabbi . . ."

"Shhh! Not here." Peter's voice stern, soft. Walking in silence. "It may not be that way."

"What do you mean?" Judas's sharp whisper.

"He doesn't seem to be ready for that."

"We will be ready for him."

Walking in silence. Peter and Judas, swirling in darkness and light. Help them. Your heart reaches out to them. They walk so fast. You reach out your hand. "Pe . . . ter."

"Come along, Jotham." Swirling in darkness and light. Walking so fast.

"Come on, Jotham." Mary reaches to take your hand. Smiling. In her smile is Abba's light.

"THE TEMPLE, Jotham."

You stand looking at broad stone steps, a large court, a wall beyond. What is it that frightens you? Fear. Like standing on a high cliff looking down, down. Like stories your mother told you of lions, huge and golden-skinned, knife-toothed. "The lion will get you, Jotham, if . . ."

"Come on, Jotham," Mary says.

What is there is like the light, but so big you can't see it. Big, big. You feel it touching you inside, deep in your heart, hurting, hurting. An eye inside of fire, and you are afraid.

"Come on!" A hand on your arm. Impatient.

You climb the steps slowly. Up and down, your feet go up

and down, slowly, reluctantly. Your voice wants to speak but it cannot. You open your mouth.

"Yi . . . rah . . . yi . . . rah."

"What's wrong with him?" Judas asks.

Peter looks at you. "Is he afraid?"

You walk into the court. Men are there. Men with trays and stalls. Men talking, laughing, arguing, bargaining. They do not see the thing that is there. Children playing by a high cliff. Children playing, playing while the lion stalks close, huge and golden-skinned, knife-toothed. "The lion . . ."

Abba.

He stands in the middle of the court. His light is glowing sharp, knife sharp, like the lion's teeth. He is angry. You cringe, but you know he is not angry with you. You watch. He walks to one of the stalls and takes hold of it with his strong hands. Far away, but you see his muscles tense, feel his anger, see him clearly. Fire and water, muscle and sweat, and all the other men are ghosts. He seizes the stall and throws it to the ground.

"Aahh . . ."

Silence flows from the ghosts like wind. He walks to another stall and seizes it. Ghost hands reach out to stop him, but they cannot hold him.

"Aahh . . ."

He throws the stall to the ground and seizes another. He throws that one down, and another and another. Ghost voices crying out. Rattling, Rattling. Dead men's throats, empty wind.

"Aahh . . ."

He strides to the center of the court and stands. Legs apart, fists on his hips. Strong. Ghosts flutter around, afraid, outraged.

He stands clear. Clear and still and strong.

Hush.

Ghosts flutter, whisper, whisper.

Abba's voice, fire and bronze.

"You've turned my father's house into a den of thieves!"

TIRED.

All afternoon you sit on the ground, your back against the wall, listening to the women inside preparing the meal. Hushed voices. Sound of knives and clay pots.

Growing shadows. Coolness. Drifting.

"Jotham!" Woman's voice. A hand shakes you.

"Let him sleep." Mary's voice. "I'll do it."

"He's useless."

"He's tired. He's never seen so much, all at once."

Coolness. Drifting. Your head cradled in your arms on the ground. Drifting.

"Do you want to eat, Jotham?" Mary's voice. Drifting. Drifting.

Sleep. Long, jagged dreams. Long, dusty road. Your feet go up and down, up and down, up and down.

Faces. "Why would your rabbi bring along a big child like that?" Hot sunlight. "Jo . . . tham. Idiot boy. Stupid as a donkey."

Darkness. Old Abba in your old house, sitting at the table. You put your hand on his shoulder. He stands up, looks at you, turns away.

Abba!

Your eyes open. In the dark, new Abba crouches beside you. His eyes look at your eyes, look deep inside.

The light. Strong but dim. In it a fear you've never seen. A fear so great that it makes you afraid.

New Abba reaches out. His strong hand on your shoulder. Calm. Calm.

"Jotham." His voice whispers.

"I know what you've dreamed, Jotham. I too have had this dream."

Silence. Abba crouches beside you in the darkness, his hand on your shoulder, his eyes deep in your eyes.

The light. Strong but dim. It flickers with the fear you've never seen there, the fear that makes you afraid.

You tremble. "Yi . . . rah . . . yi . . . rah."

"Calm, Jotham. Calm." The strong hand on your shoulder. Calm. Calm.

The light, stronger, stronger, fighting back the fear. The fear flickering, weaker, weaker.

"Rabbi." Peter's voice. "Should we go?"

A moment. Abba squeezes your shoulder. He stands up.

"Good night, Jotham. Sleep."

Peter and several others. Abba joins them. They start walking. The light among pale shapes.

Calm. You are calm, watching the light. Then in the light you suddenly see a bright red gash of fear.

PEOPLE.

Men and women crowding against you. Their anger spits at you.

"Out of the way, boy!"

"Get the idiot out of there!"

"Someone should take him away."

You push up against a wall. People rush by. Your eyes watch their faces. Old, young, angry, worried, afraid.

Where is the light?

Hot morning sun. Sweat. People. Voices shouting, arguing, whining.

Close your eyes and put your hands over your ears. Hot, dark, muffled sounds. Quiet. Quiet. You begin to see the light. Dim, glowing. The red gash of fear. Scarred over like a wound. Scarred over with pain. Need. Abba needs you.

Drop your hands. Open your eyes. The people rush back. Sunlight. Noise. But now you know where to go.

You step away from the wall, into the crowd.

"Watch where you're going, fool!"

A hand pushes you. Stumbling. Your hand scrapes the wall,

your knee hits the paving stone. Blood. Laughter.

The light. You clamber up and stand. You start forward.

"Idiot!"

A leg catches at your feet, a hand pushes. You fall. Laughter. Your head hits the paving stone. Warm blood, blurring your eyes. Laughter.

"Leave him alone." Woman's voice. A strong, thin hand on your shoulder.

Turn your head. Old woman's face, thin. Deep brown eyes. Damp cloth on your face. Peaceful, cooling.

"It's only a simpleton, Mama." A young voice, behind the old woman.

"I know." The old face speaks. Woman's voice. "Can you stand?"

Her strong, thin hand on your arm. You struggle up. Stand. Dizzy. Strong, thin hand.

"Can you walk?"

"Ab . . . Ab . . . ba."

"He doesn't know what he's saying, Mama. Be careful. Let's go."

"Can you walk?" the old woman asks again.

The light.

"Let's go, Mama. Look how big he is . . ."

The light. You stumble forward, walking, walking. Walking toward the light. Up and down. Lift your foot, set it down, lift your other foot. Walking.

Her strong, thin hand is gone.

A wide street. Afternoon sun. Horses. Donkeys. People pressing against you.

People drifting apart, a space around you.

"Aside!"

"Aah!" Your lips scream pain.

Stumbling forward. Fire pain on your back. A hundred knife blades cutting your shoulders. You look up.

Tall foreigners on horses. Whips. Helmets, breastplates. Riding by. Two horses pulling two wheels. A cold, distant face. Its eyes fall on you. Eyes are handsome, far away, cruel.

You turn, running. Blood on your back, warm, oozing. Blood on your hand, blood on your knee. Bumping against a man. He pushes. Anger. Abba! Light.

Crowds. You stop running. People, people. An open area. Up hill. You step on a loose stone. Falling. Flat. You lie. Tired, alone. Your eyes close against the ground.

"Are you all right?"

Man's voice. You turn your head. A stranger. Dark face, white cloth on his head.

"Let me help you."

You lie. Then the light calls you. Reaches your heart. You try to get up. A big hand under your arm, helping. You stand. Then, far away, over the heads of the people, you see Abba. Dying. Hanging against the sky.

Abba! Abba!

You struggle forward, your body filled with pain.

Abba! "Abba!"

The backs and shoulders of people stop you. You push against them. They push and hold you back.

The light flickering.

"Abba!"

Sudden darkness inside you. Sky trembles. Your body trembles. Your heart rips in two, ripping pain. Sudden red gash.

Your insides turn pitch black. Hurt. Pain.

Tears stream down your cheeks. Legs trembling. You fall to the dirt.

Darkness.

Abba.

❁❁

NIGHT.

The stones of the empty streets weep. Silently. Crying out in soundless pain.

The walls of the houses echo the sound of your feet. Lonely sound: a stone dropped in a well.

Darkness.

You walk up and down the streets. The hills, the curving alleys. You pass a beggar huddled in the dark. His voice whines quietly toward you, hopeless and empty, a shepherd's flute playing a song in the desert.

Oh the streets are dark! The stars in blue-black sky are cold and far away.

A door opens. A rectangle of light falls at your feet. You jump back. Afraid. No one comes out of the house. No voices. You wait, heart thumping. The rectangle of light lies in front of you, blocking your way. Like a snake in front of you, yellow and horrible. You creep slowly and carefully to the far side of the street. Sweating. A narrow strip of darkness, safe against the far wall.

You edge by the bright rectangle. Sweating. You pass it and walk down the street. Afraid, you look back. The rectangle is gone.

Darkness in the dark. You look up. A high wall at the turning of an alley blocks out the sky.

The temple. Light so light you are blind to it. Darkness so deep it is terror. You stand frozen. Oh Abba, Abba, what is this light I can't see? Where are you, Abba? Tears running down your face. "Abba!" your voice yells. "Abba . . . Abba . . ." Your voice bounces off the dark stone street.

You stop, panting.

You've been running. Sweat covers your body. Good, sweat. You are alone in dark streets, winding around. You do not know where you are, yet you suddenly know.

You are being sent now. Sent to find someone. You know it, and you walk, walk. At a corner you pause, then know the right way. Again and again this happens, until you find dirt under your feet and the houses farther apart. You come to a long, low wall.

Then you see him, huddled in a corner. A mass of gray and darkness. You walk to him. He is facing away.

"Ju . . . das."

He whips around and looks at you. His gray eyes startled, scared in the dark.

"Jotham." Almost a spit. Almost a whisper.

He looks long at you. Then he laughs. Dry, empty laugh. He puts his hand on your shoulder.

"Are you too stupid to know?"

His gray eyes watching you. Gray eyes trapped in light and darkness.

"Ju . . . das." Your heart calling him. Calling. Calling into his gray eyes. Light and dark struggling in his eyes. Your heart reaching toward him. Reaching, trying to touch.

"You're a fool, Jotham." His voice soft. His hand drops from your shoulder. He takes his eyes away from your eyes.

Judas, Judas. Your heart reaching. "Ju . . . das."

"You fool!" He turns on you. Angry. Eyes flashing darkness. "Get away from me." His eyes, dark and hard, staring into your eyes. He rips them away and is gone.

Emptiness. The darkness in his eyes. A knife inside you cutting, cutting your stomach and chest. Your body cut open, your heart throbbing against the night air.

"Ju . . . das!"

Tears running down your face.

EYES OPEN.

Night dreams fill you with emptiness. Afraid.

Pale sky. Cold.

You are in a place of few houses, huddled against a stone wall. Sharp stones, hard dirt.

Abba gone.

Sun rising. Morning.

Darkness over the pale sky.

Stand up.

Hungry. Empty pain in your stomach.

A road going toward the sun.

You walk. Up and down your feet go. You watch your feet. Up and down. Up and down.

The sun bigger, brighter. Starting to pierce the day with heat.

Darkness over the bright sky.

"Boy!"

Look up.

A tall man in dark clothing. Straight. Sharp brown eyes. Servant beside him.

Purse jingles. White hand to servant hand.

"Give him this."

Servant walks toward you. Quick, raven eyes. Three coins in his callused palm.

"Take this." He gives you one coin. His hand slips softly to his belt. The other coins disappear.

He smiles.

The coin. You hold it tight, your hand sweating over it. Up and down your feet go. You feel your heart thumping around the hard sharpness of the coin in your hand.

Hungry. Empty pains.

Bread. Old woman with bread. Walk to her.

"Where's your money?"

You open your hand. The coin is gone.

Your heart empty inside you. You look at your sweating palm. The mark of the coin on your hand. No coin. You look up.

The bread woman laughs and walks away.

You look at the ground. Where is the coin? You walk back, looking, looking. Careless boy. Looking, looking. Head hurting, heart hurting. Empty hunting. Rocks, stones, brush, dirt, pebbles. The sun growing cool. Looking, looking. Foolish boy. Beside that rock. Yes! No.

Only shadows. Shadows. Shadows growing larger. Eyes aching, back aching. Tears on your face.

You find a place. Safe place against a rock. Sit. Tears. Hunger. Aching. Stupid boy.

Cool air. Stars.

Darkness over the starlit sky.

DARK DREAMS.

You fall in your sleep. A stone in a deep well. Open your mouth and scream. Soundless scream.

Pitch dark. Alone. Forever. Eyes cannot see. Ears cannot hear. Black silence closing in on you. Your head in a small dark hole. No air. Your lungs ache.

Abba!

Abba walking alone. The light glowing hard and intense in the darkness. Alone.

Darkness so dark. It swallows the light faster than the light flows from Abba. The light dimming, flickering, growing smaller. The hungry dark, eating, eating the light.

Abba! Abba! Your heart reaches out. Abba! Abba! Abba! All alone in hungry darkness. The light smaller and smaller. Intense and hard. Smaller. Bright. Smaller. No air. Lungs ache. You want to breathe. Abba! You scream with no sound.

The light explodes and grows, shining. Abba lifts his arms, his voice, lifting his face upward, his eyes, his lips. Calling soundlessly, light growing and growing. Touching you, reaching you. Sunlight in the well, good light. Life.

Growing, growing light, pushing the darkness, beating it back. Growing light flowing over you.

"Jotham! Jotham!"

A hand shaking you.

"Jotham! Wake up!" Mary's voice.

The light glowing in Mary's voice. Golden bright. Abba light.

"Jotham!"

You open your eyes. You are in the country, alone, far from town. No one is near. Dawn breaking. Pale yellow sky. Cool air. Silence. You look around.

"Ma . . . ry?"

You turn in circles. Lost, lost. Like the lost coin. Your head is confused. You stand and stare, looking down a hill, along the road.

No Mary. She is not there. You are alone.

Far down the road, a figure moving. Coming closer. Not light, not darkness. Closer. Rugged clothes. Not peace, not danger. You look down at the ground, at your feet, then up again. An ordinary man, a stranger, coming closer. You watch him. Closer. His eyes on you.

He stoops over and picks up a clump of earth and wild grass from the ground. "Jotham!" He swings his arm. Graceful. Radiant. The clump sails through the air toward you.

"Abba!"

Your eyes see him clearly. Your feet move forward slowly, up and down. He is running toward you, laughing.

"Abba!"

"Jotham!" Abba's voice, laughing. His arms around you. Holding you. Your head on his chest. Deep laughing inside.

"Did I surprise you?"

Your face smiling. Abba so big. You are in his arms, long ago in Mama's arms. Your arms around him, feeling his warmth and strength.

"Jotham, Jotham." Your name. Quiet, deep voice. His arms tighten around you. Safe. Warm. His tunic, the long, bright, sand-colored road, the sun standing still.

A strong, tight hug. Then he is gone.

Gone. You can't see him. You stand, peaceful. Not lost. No lost coin.

❀❀

SUN CLIMBING THE SKY. Yellow in blue. You turn back along the road, back to Peter, Thomas, Mary. Up and down you walk, slow feet, heart dancing, up and down. Up and down, up and down, sun climbing, yellow and blue, houses, closer and closer, people.

"Jotham!"

Look up. Mary running toward you. Light in her face, smiling.

"Jotham!"

Your heart beats in you, dancing, up and down, up and down.

Abba's golden light. Her arms around you.

"Come along, Jotham." Smiles in Mary's voice.

"We've seen him! The rabbi's alive!"

ABBA. WITH YOU MANY DAYS. With Peter, Mary, Thomas. Now gone again.

But not gone as before. This time, you might see him if you turn around. Turn around quickly. Light there, but not there. Abba there, but not there. You laugh. Like a game with your sister when you were little. Adina hiding behind the house, behind the wall. Turning to see her. She's gone. You laugh.

"Come on, Jotham." Laughter in Mary's voice. You follow her along a narrow street. Men, women, children bumping against you. Wooden stalls. Cloth, meat, fruit. Loud voices.

"Jotham," a voice whispers. You turn quickly. Light there, but not there. Abba there, but not there.

You laugh.

Gray. Gray.

Sometimes Abba hides from you and makes you laugh. Sometimes he's gone far away.

Lonely, dull heart. Gray. Dead branches. Dead branch on an olive tree.

"Cut it down," old Abba said.

"Let it be, let me try a little longer," Mama said. Long ago. Far away.

New Abba gone again. No. Not gone. Mary says not gone. Far away. Far away.

Morning.

Your heart quiet, suddenly leaps in you. Dances in you. Sings in you.

"Ma . . . ry."

She turns. Fire. She wipes her hands. Many women.

"What does he want?" a woman asks.

"I don't know. What do you want, Jotham?"

"Ma . . . ry." Your heart dances. Your feet dance. You laugh. You pull her hand.

"Something's wrong with him," the woman says.

"No. He wants me to go with him." Mary's voice ripples like a pond. Deep, living water.

You pull her hand. She follows. Your heart knows where to go. Up and down your feet dance. Up and down. You lead her through the courtyard and around corners. Up a stairway. Your feet dancing, your heart dancing. Up the stairs. Stone stairs in sunlight. Gray stones, hard, worn, happy. Up the stairs into the room.

Hush. Your heart dances. Your body stills. Peter is there. Thomas. Abba's mother. Many, many people. Silent, sitting. Calm and quiet. Mary beside you, silent, holding your hand, looking with wide eyes.

Sudden loud, rushing wind.

Light. Light. Light dancing. Dancing over Peter's head, over Thomas, over Abba's mother. Light. Light, dancing over Mary. Dancing.

"Jotham."

"Ab . . . ba!" Light exploding inside of you, beautiful. Close your eyes. Light inside you, flowing like living water.

"Jotham."

Your heart opens. Praise him, praise him. Your lips open. Praise him! Praise God! Glory to God in the highest. Praise him sun and moon, earth and stars, praise him. Blessed is he who comes in the name of the Lord!

"Jotham.

Strong hand on your shoulder. Open your eyes. Peter.

"Pe . . . ter."

He smiles and steps by you, out the door. Follow him. Up and down your feet go. Stop. Look down.

The street below. People dancing, laughing, praising. People. Many people coming. Light. Light paling the sun. You laugh.

Close your eyes.

"Jotham."

Gentle voice. Abba. Inside you. Filling you inside with light. You laugh. Abba laughs.

Up and down, your heart dances. Up and down.

"Ab . . . ba!" your lips slowly say.

"Jotham," Abba answers. Inside you. Beautiful light, flowing like water.

"Jotham."

Abba with you. This time for always.

Light. Light. Light.

Author's Note

I have been asked to write a few words about *The Book of Jotham:* how it came to be written, and where it has been for twenty-three years. It is a daunting task that has deep roots, and it involves, initially, three dates, each ten years apart.

In 1969, I entered the Peace Corps. It was something I had dreamed of doing since President Kennedy founded the Peace Corps, but I admit that I was spurred to it by the imminent threat of being drafted to Vietnam. Twenty-one years old, I had done very well academically, graduating with distinction from Shimer College—a challenging Great Books offshoot of the University of Chicago—and I completed my first year at Harvard Law School before the government did away with draft deferments for graduate students. I was cocky, not a little conceited, and (as my mother would have put it) thought I was the cat's pajamas.

The Peace Corps sent me to Brazil. It was an incredibly valuable experience, not least because I was forced to face my own limits. No native linguist, I struggled with Portuguese. For six months, I had the vocabulary of a four-year-old. For at least a year after that, although I could get by on a work level, it was extremely difficult for me to express complex or nuanced thoughts. I had always been articulate. Suddenly, however, I was forced to be quiet and listen.

I arrived in Brazil an agnostic, seemingly the only rational religious position. In Brazil, I worked closely with people whose faith was woven into their lives, who had vivid experiences with what we North Americans consider to be the supernatural. My agnostic faith—and with it my whole rationalistic worldview—was called into question.

In 1971, I met Brenda King, a newly arrived Peace Corps volunteer in the Brazilian state of Bahia. We fell in love, became engaged, and had many adventures together in romantic, tropical Bahia. In 1973, we returned to the United States, where we were married, and I went back to law school, graduating in 1975. Brenda has been a lifelong Catholic. I participated at church with her, and on Easter Vigil 1976, when I was twenty-nine years old, I was baptized and entered the Roman Catholic Church.

By 1979, we were again living in Brazil, in Rio de Janeiro, where I had accepted a job with a prestigious international law firm. Brenda, who had completed her master's in pastoral studies at Loyola University Chicago, was working as a community organizer in the Rio slums. We would go out to dinner with my American and Canadian clients, and mention to them that the chambermaids in Brenda's women's groups, who worked in the hotels where my clients stayed, earned less for a month of work than my clients paid for a night's stay.

Working in this manner opened our eyes in many ways. As Peace Corps volunteers, we had lived with the poor. Now we began to understand more fully the structures that—often, unintentionally—created and perpetuated poverty. We hungered to work more closely with the Church in helping the poor—a hunger that was to bear fruit six years later.

Also in 1979, we adopted our first daughter, Ana Cristina. As part of her job, Brenda visited orphanages. One day, at an orphanage in São Gonçalo, outside of Rio, she felt a tug on her skirt, looked down, and saw a two-year-old child looking up at her. She knew immediately that we were meant to adopt this child. It took nearly a year of winding our way through the court system, but on October 1, 1979, Ana Cristina was in our custody.

It was that year when Jotham was born. In the preface, I mention that he was born out of a deep concern about the mentally challenged and their role in God's plan. As with most such concerns, its roots went deep: our Down syndrome neighbor when I was a child (a girl who was kept in an institution and rarely seen when at home, yet friendly and always happy); my grandmother's Alzheimer's disease; and many encounters since. Converting to Christianity, I accepted that the mentally challenged are God's children, but why are they born so? As Thomas says in *The Book of Jotham*, "I don't see why all the pots can't be strong and beautiful."

There was, of course, in those days as there is today, a great deal of talk about abortion and quality of life. I found the secular vision of these to be inherently wrong, and yet I couldn't really give voice to my reasons. Part of my problem, I came to realize, was that I focused my own identity—my own sense of value—on my mind, on my intelligence. Yet intelligence (I thought of my grandmother and of many other elders) is a fragile, temporary thing. This was scary to me.

Mentally challenged people thus embodied a question for me—one that frightened me, because it put into question my very sense of self. It was this question I brought to prayer, and this question that was answered one morning in Our Lady of Mercy Chapel. It was not really answered, but, as God so often does, given as a story: *The Book of Jotham.*

Yet it wasn't until ten years later, in 1989, that I completed writing *The Book of Jotham*. That is not surprising. God plants seeds and they grow slowly. In this case, much had occurred in those ten years that was necessary to my spiritual growth.

In 1983, we adopted our second daughter, Angelica. Her adoption is a miraculous story, one that I hope to share some day.

In 1985, Brenda and I received an invitation from the Franciscans (Holy Name Province) to work with them in the eastern Amazon region, in what is now the state of Tocantins. The friars were responsible for an area around the village of Caseara, on the Araguaia River, but this region was very difficult for them to reach. In addition to their pastoral needs, the rural people's land was becoming more valuable. The small farmers in the region were threatened with *grilagem,* the use of fraud and force to remove them from their land. It was a violent region. The murder, in 1986, of Father Josimo Tavares and, years later, across the river in Pará, of Sister Dorothy Stang were the most notorious of many killings. Two farmers we worked with were murdered, and our lives were threatened several times.

Brenda and I did pastoral work: working with couples, families, youth; promoting community education, sacramental preparation, Bible studies. We also helped organize subsistence farmers' and rural workers' unions. We stayed in Tocantins for seven years.

It was only in 1989, when we went on home leave, that we realized the tension under which we were living. I remember sitting on my parents' screened porch in Safety Harbor, Florida, when a pickup truck drove into the parking lot next door. I leaped to my feet. In Tocantins, pickup trucks could mean danger.

Later, during that home leave, I completed *The Book of Jotham.* The story, given to me, grew organically. I read widely—the work of Jean Vanier and the L'Arche communities especially touched me. We had lived and read scripture among a rural people who heard the Bible stories much the way Jesus's listeners must have heard them. The Franciscans had sent us on a tour of the Holy Land with Father Steven Doyle, OFM, a wonderful biblical scholar. Both in mission and at home, we had grown to know families with mentally challenged members, who are (as Jean Vanier taught) gifts from God.

All the artists I know have the sense that, at least in their best work, something is flowing through them. A purely secular artist might claim that this flow comes from his or her own subconscious. There is some truth in this—certainly, over the years, our minds fill with myriad experiences that we draw upon as artists. Yet most artists, even those who are not particularly religious, seem to feel that there is some greater inspiration for their work—that something greater is flowing through them. We are craftsmen, and we know our craft is important, but stories have a life of their own, characters come alive and seize the direction of a story. Words flow from us in ways we never could have imagined. Looking back at our best work, we can say "Yes, I wrote this, but the story came through me, not from me."

Part of the writer's craft is empathy. In order to write a character, I must, in a certain sense, become that character. I am Jotham, and if this story works at all, it is because you, the reader, become (for the time you are reading this book) Jotham. Becoming Jotham brought home a truth to me: We are all mentally challenged. Perhaps this is even clearer to me as I grow older and my learning patterns change, my memory fades. In the eyes of God (who loves every one of us), what real difference is there between the mental capacities of Jotham and those of Einstein? Both capacities are minuscule. St. Thomas Aquinas knew this at the end of his life. All his brilliant work appeared to him as straw.

Our years of mission and my own family life also taught me that there are many kinds of intelligence. I knew illiterate farmers who could easily remember plants, making distinctions among plants that were as opaque to me as written letters were to them. I knew a simple man who understood the ways and powers of snakes so thoroughly he could protect from harm a school full of children. I knew a woman who healed a nearly dead bird by holding a branch to it and saying a prayer. The branch withered and the bird stood and started singing. Another woman I knew saw auras around people and could tell much about their health and their needs. Our daughter Ana Cristina is an incredibly intuitive massage therapist who knows where people feel pain simply by passing her hands over them. She also has a keen sense of the presence of evil. It is not whether we are intelligent, but in what way we are intelligent. Jotham sees things others cannot see.

I've been asked how it is that *The Book of Jotham* remained essentially unknown over the years. The answer is simple: I was living in Brazil, a full-time husband and father, earning a living at highly demanding jobs, and with relatively little time to think about writing, much less about publishing.

In 1996, I was repatriated to the United States with hepatitis. At that time, I gave a copy of *The Book of Jotham* to Father Joseph Girzone, author of the *Joshua* series, and received two very encouraging letters from him. Then I returned to Rio de Janeiro and another demanding job, and *The Book of Jotham* remained in my files.

All things happen at the right time. Recent years have seen a rebirth in Catholic literature. The time has come for *The Book of Jotham* to reach out to the reading public. It is my hope that Jotham can help us all more fully understand the invaluable, unique nature of every human, every child of God.

About the Author

Arthur Powers went to Brazil in 1969 as a Peace Corps volunteer and lived most of his adult life there. From 1985 to 1992, he and his wife, Brenda, with their two daughters, served as Catholic lay missioners in eastern Amazon. Arthur subsequently directed Catholic Relief Services in Brazil. He and Brenda currently live with a daughter and granddaughter in Raleigh, North Carolina. He is on the pastoral council of St. Raphael parish, where he is active on the Social Justice Committee, a member of the Knights of Columbus, and chairman of the Diversity Committee (the parish comprises representatives from more than eighty ethnic and national groups).

Arthur was granted a fellowship in fiction from the Massachusetts Artists Foundation, three annual awards for short fiction from the Catholic Press Association, and earned second place in the 2008 Tom Howard Fiction Contest. His poetry and fiction have appeared in many magazines and anthologies, among them *America, Christianity & Literature; Dappled*

Things; Hiram Poetry Review; Liguorian; Prime Number; Roanoke Review; St. Anthony Messenger; St. Katherine Review; South Carolina Review; Southern Poetry Review; Worcester Review; and two anthologies from Editions Bibliotekos. Press 53 published *A Hero for the People,* a collection of his short stories set in Brazil.